THIS WALKER BOOK BELONGS TO:

_____

_____

_____

_____

For
Romany, Willie, Joe,
and Harry

First published in the Netherlands 1993 by
Uitgeverij J.H. Gottmer/H.J.W. Becht B.V.
Published in Great Britain 1994 by
Walker Books Ltd, 87 Vauxhall Walk, London SE11 5HJ
This edition published 1995

2 4 6 8 10 9 7 5 3 1

© 1993 Helen Oxenbury

This book has been typeset in Bembo.

Printed in Hong Kong

British Library Cataloguing in Publication Data
A catalogue record for this title is available
from the British Library.
ISBN 0-7445-4344-4

It's My Birthday

Helen Oxenbury

WALKER BOOKS
AND SUBSIDIARIES
LONDON · BOSTON · SYDNEY

"It's my birthday and
I'm going to make a cake."

"It's my birthday and
I'm going to make a cake.
I need some eggs."

"I'll get you some eggs,"
said the chicken.

"It's my birthday and
  I'm going to make a cake.
  I've got the eggs.
  But I need some flour."

"I'll get you some flour,"
  said the bear.

"It's my birthday and
  I'm going to make a cake.
  I've got the eggs and the flour.
  But I need some butter and milk."

"I'll get you some butter and milk,"
                    said the cat.

"It's my birthday and
    I'm going to make a cake.
    I've got eggs, flour, butter, and milk.
    But I need a pinch of salt."

"I'll get you a pinch of salt,"
        said the pig.

"It's my birthday and
I'm going to make a cake.
I've got eggs, flour, butter, milk,
and a pinch of salt.
But I need some sugar."

"I'll get you some sugar,"
said the dog.

"It's my birthday and
    I'm going to make a cake.
    I've got eggs, flour, butter, milk,
    a pinch of salt, and sugar.
    But I need some
    cherries for the top."

"I'll get you some cherries for the top,"
                    said the monkey.

"It's my birthday and
   I'm going to make a cake.
   I've got everything I need."

"We'll all help you make the cake,"
   said the chicken, the bear,
   the cat, the pig, the dog,
   and the monkey.

"Thank you, everybody.
Now all of you can …

… help me eat the cake!"

"Happy Birthday!"

MORE WALKER PAPERBACKS
For You to Enjoy

Growing up with Helen Oxenbury
TOM AND PIPPO

There are six stories in each of these two colourful books about toddler Tom
and his special friend Pippo, a soft-toy monkey.

"Just right for small children… A most welcome addition to the nursery shelves." *Books for Keeps*

At Home with Tom and Pippo 0-7445-3721-5
Out and About with Tom and Pippo 0-7445-3720-7
£3.99 each

THREE PICTURE STORIES

Each of the titles in this series contains three classic stories of pre-school life,
first published individually as First Picture Books.

"Everyday stories of family life, any one of these humorous depictions of the trials
of an under-five will be readily identified by children and adults …
buy them all if you can." *Books For Your Children*

One Day with Mum 0-7445-3722-3
A Bit of Dancing 0-7445-3723-1
A Really Great Time 0-7445-3724-X
£3.99 each

MINI MIX-AND-MATCH BOOKS

Originally published as Heads, Bodies and Legs, these fun-packed
little novelty books each contain 729 possible combinations!

"Good value, highly imaginative, definitely to be looked out for."
Books For Your Children

Animal Allsorts 0-7445-3705-3
Puzzle People 0-7445-3706-1
£2.99 each

Walker Paperbacks are available from most booksellers, or by post from B.B.C.S., P.O. Box 941, Hull, North Humberside HU1 3YQ

24 hour telephone credit card line 01482 224626

To order, send: Title, author, ISBN number and price for each book ordered, your full name and address,
cheque or postal order payable to BBCS for the total amount and allow the following for postage and packing:
UK and BFPO: £1.00 for the first book, and 50p for each additional book to a maximum of £3.50.
Overseas and Eire: £2.00 for the first book, £1.00 for the second and 50p for each additional book.

Prices and availability are subject to change without notice.